Little rabbit Buddy woke up on a Mor

Little rabbit went about his daily routine, he got dressed for school, had his breakfast and gave his mummy and daddy a great BIG hug before his day ahead!

Buddy enjoyed school. He had lots of friends to play and learn with. His BESTEST friend is called Dougie!

After a tiring day of adventures it was finally home time! When Buddy got home mummy and daddy asked him to sit at the table. They had some very important news... mummy rabbit explained to Buddy "You don't have to go back to school for a little while, you will be staying at home with me and daddy. We will be working here and looking after you!"

Buddy was so pleased with this news because as much as he loved school he loved time off with his family the best!
"YAY! Can we go and have a picnic at the park tomorrow? Or maybe to meet Dougie at the play area?!"

This made Buddy feel angry and confused "THAT'S NOT FAIR, I WANT TO GO AND SEE DOUGIE ... I WANT TO SEE GRANDMA AND GRANDAD OR ENJOY THE SUNSHINE AT THE PARK OR THE BEACH? PLEASE PLEASE PLEASE MUMMY? "

Mummy could understand why buddy was upset and wanted to explain to him what was going on. "Come here darling". Buddy sulked over and sat by mummy on the sofa. Mummy sighed and said "We have to stay at home for a little while now, there is a nasty bug out there making lots of people sick, we don't want to catch it, or spread it to anyone. We're safe here at home little one. "

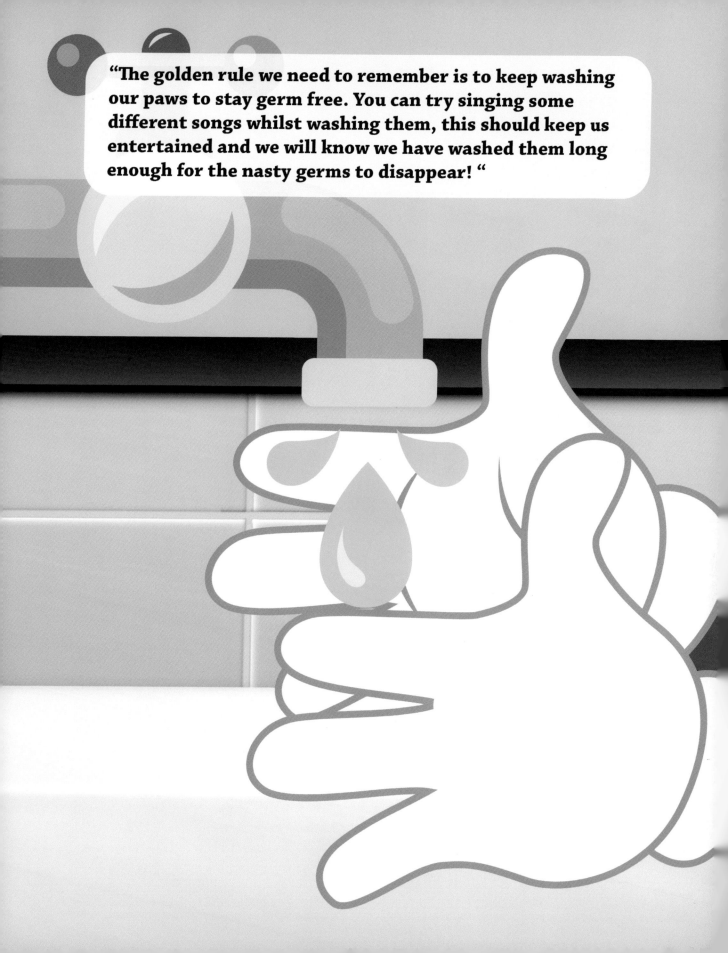

This was hard for Buddy to understand but he started to get used to his new routine day by day. The Rabbits stayed at home and did lots of fun things like ... Making rainbows for the window, going for walks to wave at grandma and grandad, Easter egg hunts, jigsaw puzzles... Buddy even learnt to write his own name!

Each week Buddy would call his family and his bestest friend Dougie. Dougie missed Buddy "I miss you so much, it's not fair my mummy and daddy are still going to work, I have to go to school and it's no fun without you!"The little friends dreamed of the day they could play together again.

Buddy couldn't understand what Dougie had told him. Daddy gave Buddy a big cuddle and said "Some rabbits still have to go to work to keep us all safe and healthy. These rabbits are very special to us. Each family is different".

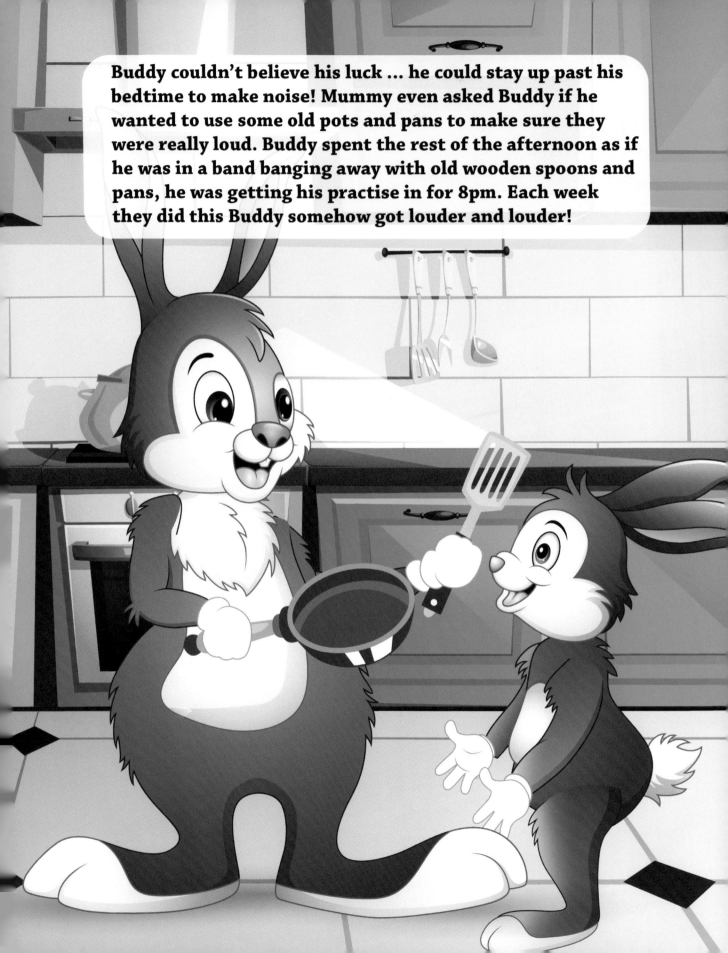

Buddy couldn't believe his luck ... he could stay up past his bedtime to make noise! Mummy even asked Buddy if he wanted to use some old pots and pans to make sure they were really loud. Buddy spent the rest of the afternoon as if he was in a band banging away with old wooden spoons and pans, he was getting his practise in for 8pm. Each week they did this Buddy somehow got louder and louder!

It was a few months later and things were finally starting to go back to normal, schools were opening.

Mummy and daddy's could go back to work and lucky for Buddy the play areas were starting to open once again.

Buddy went back to school and loved seeing everyone and talking about what they had been up to during their time at home! Some rabbits had new hair styles and learnt new tricks. Some rabbits were a little shy and nervous about returning back to bunny school.

Mummy picked Buddy up at hometime and they had a picnic tea at the park with best friend Dougie. Grandma and Grandad even joined them and kindly bought some delicious carrot cake! This day felt so special and exciting.

By the end of the week Buddy and his family felt very tired but happy that everything was back to normal. Mummy was reading Buddy a bedtime story and asked "Now dear, what shall we do this weekend? Shall we go to the park? The beach? The library? Grandma and grandad's?"

The rabbits enjoyed everything in life much more than they did before. Every trip out was never taken for granted again and the littlest treats seemed much more special. When family life returned back to normal the little family of rabbits made sure they still carried on all the fun and laughter at home making new memories each day!

The End

we hope you enjoyed this story.

Here are some questions you can ask yourself, your family and your friends.

What is your favourite activity to do at home?

Where are you most excited to visit when everywhere opens again?

Who are you most excited to play with again?

How are you feeling?

Printed in Poland
by Amazon Fulfillment
Poland Sp. z o.o., Wrocław